Flames of Freedom

Thomas S. Owens
AR B.L.: 3.2
Points: 1.0

MG

Flames of Freedom

by Thomas S. Owens

Perfection Learning®

Cover Illustration: Pat Muchmore
Inside Illustration: Pat Muchmore

Dedication
To Eunice Blackburn

About the Author
Thomas S. Owens is married to Diana Star Helmer, another author of children's books. Thomas is the author of more than 40 books, including *Collecting Basketball Cards* (Millbrook Press). He likes walking with Diana, cooking soups, gardening, watching cartoons, surfing the Internet, playing with Angel the cat, and living in Iowa.

Image credits: Art Today pp. 9, 10, 12, 13, 20, 23, 27, 28, 29, 31, 32, 33, 35, 37, 42, 44, 46, 47, 48, 50, 51, 52, 53; Corel p. 11, 14

Table of Contents

Chapter 1

The Night Raid

"Burn, Tories! Burn!"

The shout rang through the three-room home. Timothy Lyman was jarred awake. The 11-year-old sat straight up in his feather bed.

Why was the sun so bright at this odd hour? Hadn't sleep just begun?

The light was firelight. It lit up the darkness around the Lyman home. An orange glow shone in the family's only window.

Smoke burned Timothy's nose. He dropped to the floor.

"Ma! Pa!" Timothy cried. "Hurry!"

Only laughter cut through the smoke. But the laughs were new to Timothy's ears.

"Come out, Tory trash!" teased a voice from the flickers of light. "Or remain in the flames of your shame!"

"Follow me!" Timothy yelled. He hoped his parents would crawl after him on the floor.

At the back door, Timothy leaped to run. But he bounced off a human. Then he felt someone shove him.

"Run back to Britain, you scoundrel!" snarled a voice.

Other human

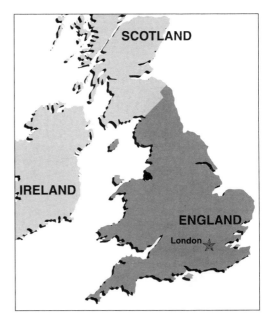

forms ringed the Lyman house. Smoke and flames danced from the circle's middle.

"Huzzah! Freedom burns brightly!" called one male.

Timothy ran down the road leading to Watertown. He found a small cottage beside the town church.

Timothy banged on the splintered wood door. He hoped the house of worship would be a safe spot.

Timothy hoped his parents would follow. Someday, they might laugh at all this. At being mistaken for foes of freedom.

"Please, I need shelter! Someone! Offer me refuge. Your floor. Anywhere!" Timothy's whispers seemed loud.

He kept looking over his shoulder.

Would the shadows turn into unknown enemies?

"Who calls at the devil's hour?" A male voice growled from behind the door.

"I am but a boy! My name is . . ."

Timothy's plea was cut short with a single "Quiet!" The heavy door inched open. An arm appeared. It pointed toward another building.

"The barn may be yours for tonight. Stay if you must."

One last slam was the final reply to Timothy's plea.

Timothy spied the building. It looked like a twin to the parson's home.

He staggered to the barn. The moon shone on the foggy steam coming from the cow's nose.

The cow seemed to fill half the space. Hay beds surrounded the beast.

Timothy fell into a welcoming straw pile. He was far from the cow. And he was far from his family. Tears streaked his soot-covered face. Only sleep could still his sobs.

★　★　★　★　★

"Wake up! Snap to, boy!"

He heard footsteps and a booming voice. They did not belong to the cow.

Timothy's short sleep had been filled with nightmares, screams, and smoke. There were flames and hate. Now that Timothy was awake, his nightmare was no less real.

A single candle blinked in the barn. Parson Horace Worthy stood close by. He had a shovel in each hand.

Chapter 2

Rest Not

"Follow me, young Lyman. We have much work before us. Two graves are needed before sunrise. No one wishes to dig. So we must make haste."

By fading moonlight and one lantern, the man and boy dug. Once, Timothy whispered, "Please, Parson. Tell me what happened."

The parson frowned. The boy

became silent. "Not now. Keep digging!" he hissed.

Timothy remembered townsfolk worrying about the dead. Some talked of disease spreading from the bones of the ill.

This must be the panic, Timothy thought.

A silent wave of the parson's hand stopped Timothy's digging. With another wave, the man led the boy to a wagon.

"Quickly, boy. Help me lower these departed ones into their graves."

Timothy followed orders. The bodies were wrapped in scratchy burlap flour sacks. They were adults. He could tell by their size.

"But they have no pine boxes," Timothy said.

"We have no time for such blessings," the parson replied.

Blade by blade, they returned dirt into the holes. A rooster cried far away. The sun peeked over the church steeple.

"Thank you for your help," the parson puffed. "Bow your head with me. We must pray and say good-bye to your ma and pa."

Shocked, Timothy fell to his knees. He pounded the earth. He opened his mouth. But no scream was left. The only word the boy heard was "Amen."

Parson Worthy knelt beside Timothy. He said, "You know your parents were faithful to England. Many townsfolk feared anyone who was against change. They wanted to frighten your family into supporting freedom."

Timothy shook his head in protest. Tears flew from side to side. "But they hurt no one. Why must they die?"

The parson bit his lip. "Master Lyman, no one knows such answers. In times of war, no answer seems sound.

"I only know that I had to borrow a wagon in secret. I needed it to fetch their bodies here. Their graves shall remain secret. The anger against England could be cast upon their remains. Pray they rest quiet. And in peace."

Chapter 3

Hated and Hunted

$\mathcal{S}$hock mixed with the sadness in Timothy's heart. He had not known his parents' beliefs. He had not known how they felt about taxes and kings.

But how could any beliefs be important enough to hate someone in life or in death?

And would he be hated too? Would angry rebels do worse to him?

The thunder and dust of horses roared toward the graveyard.

"Is that the runt offspring of the Lymans? Those bootlickers of Britain?" yelled a rider. He moved the rifle slung over his back.

The parson stopped the riders with one raised hand. He put his arm firmly around Timothy's shoulder.

"I have taken charge of the Tory boy," he called. "This youth will be no enemy to freedom. You have my word."

Timothy sighed. He was grateful to the parson. But then the parson's grip became overpowering.

"Citizens," the parson continued. "This Lyman will repay all of us. He will be a servant to the church!"

The horsemen pointed and laughed. Timothy knew none of them. Yet, the men eyed him with hate. Timothy had never dreamed of such hate.

"Into the church, Lyman. And await orders. Now!" the parson barked.

Timothy feared speaking out. He was small and outnumbered. He just hung his head and dashed for the church door.

Could he escape? Where would he go?

Timothy remembered a time last year in 1776. His father had spoken of going to Canada.

British officers had just ended their "watch" of Boston. Some 10,000 loyal British had gone to Nova Scotia.

These citizens wanted no part of a new government. They wanted England's support. And they wanted promises of food and protection.

Had Timothy's parents shared their feelings? Had they spoken too close to the wrong ears?

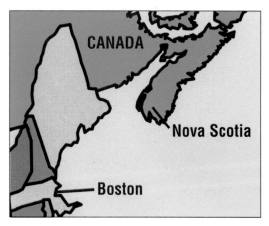

After all, Boston was less than ten miles away. Wishes for revenge could spread quickly.

Timothy did not know where else to turn. Hate could spring from behind any tree or from around any corner. For now, Timothy would be safe in the church.

He listened through the door. At last, the hoofbeats headed into the woods.

"Get away from that door!" ordered a woman's voice. "Do not even think of running. Your future is not out there."

His mother never used words with such power. The voice came from a

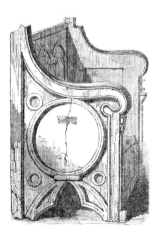

pew across the church. "I am the parson's wife. Prudence Worthy. Let us discuss how you might survive."

Chapter 4

A Surprising Woman

Timothy squeezed a fist. He tried to stare down his newest enemy. But Prudence Worthy ignored his glare.

"This is for your safety," she said. "Your stay must look different than the truth."

Timothy squinted at the woman. What did she mean?

Mrs. Worthy was sitting in the shadows. Timothy could see that she was younger than the parson. Still, her pulled-back hair held streaks of silver.

The woman folded her rough hands together. She placed them below her chin. She looked like she might pray. But instead, she looked at the boy. "Young man, do you think we have taken ownership of you?"

Timothy growled. "Call me a servant. Call me a slave. I have few choices in life right now."

Mrs. Worthy snorted. "Silly child! The point is that you must look as if you are being punished.

"The mob must not think you are being treated as an honored visitor. Or they may end your stay rudely. Need I say more?"

Timothy surprised himself by smiling. He did not remember the last time he had smiled.

"You wish to trick the villagers?" he asked. "You, the town's holy woman?"

Timothy's parents had never attended church. They had worked

hard and long on
their tiny farm.
Timothy could
only imagine how
honest the church
family was.

"Let us say that you and I will serve
a greater good in time," Mrs. Worthy
said. "And the trick may do us all some
good. I need help with my sewing. And
here you are."

She pointed to a pile of red cloth.
"Use the shears to cut strips. Match
the one I have saved."

Timothy unrolled the strip. He
thought it looked like a kite tail. Then
he saw Mrs. Worthy was measuring
blue rectangles.

"Ah!" Timothy said. "You wish to
make a flag. You want to make the flag
of our country. A Union Jack.
Correct?"

Mrs. Worthy's laugh surprised them both. "Yes and no," she answered.

"On June 14, 1777, our new Congress chose a new flag. A passerby from Boston drew the picture for me. Not the British flag. But the flag for us. For our United States!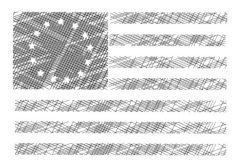

"We will have a mix of red and white stripes. Thirteen in all. One for each colony. And stars. A circle of thirteen stars."

Timothy looked closer at the red cloth he cut. He was cutting the jacket of a British officer. The ripped jacket front was stained. It wasn't dirt. It was blood!

Chapter 5

A Rebel Demand

$\mathscr{T}$imothy dropped the bloodstained coat. He stared at Mrs. Worthy. Had the parson's wife helped kill a British officer?

Mrs. Worthy answered the question in Timothy's eyes. "Wounded from both sides look to us for care and love. We could not nurse that man back to health," she said.

Timothy nodded. "Do you hate the redcoats?"

Mrs. Worthy gasped. "There is no

room for hate in my life!" she said. "If we frown upon anything, it is British rule. It stops its people from a full life.

"Taxes take food from the mouths of colonists. We have no say in the future of this land. We are puppets. And Britain pulls our strings. We ask only to break those strings."

Mrs. Worthy never looked at Timothy. She sewed with speed. She glanced often at the new flag drawing.

"We must hurry," she said. "Families will soon visit. The womenfolk will sew more flags. They will use our work as a model."

By nightfall, the Worthy home was ringed by horses and wagons. Inside, voices remained low.

Timothy stayed with Mrs. Worthy. He met other women from the village.

Two women unfurled the flag as Mrs. Worthy spoke. "The Continental Congress says that white is for goodness. Red is strength and bravery. And blue is determination and justice."

Then she said that Timothy had helped cut cloth for the flag. His face glowed a warm red. The women clapped for him.

"Timothy, Parson Worthy has left to serve an ill neighbor," Mrs. Worthy said. "Please draw fresh water from the well. Then go to the church to offer it to the men."

Timothy knew the angry faces of the riders from that morning. He hoped they would smile to see him working hard.

Mrs. Worthy had promised him safety. And he believed her.

Timothy paused at the church door with his full bucket. One man stood near the pulpit. He was trying to calm other voices.

The quiet ended when one man cried, "I say those Lymans earned such fate!"

Timothy's bucket crashed to the floor. The crowd twisted in their seats. Timothy felt his stomach jump. But his feet did not move.

"I . . . I am sorry, gentlemen!" Timothy stammered. "I will fetch you more drink."

The shouting man drew near. "Halt, Lyman boy!" he ordered. "We want more than your water."

Chapter 6

Join or Die

*S*trong hands reached for Timothy. They pulled him into the air. He was carried to the front of the church.

These might be the hands that killed my parents, Timothy thought.

A laugh boomed from the man who carried Timothy.

"Call me Patriot Paul," he chuckled.

The man wiped what looked like ashes from his sleeve. Spit, sweat, and soot speckled the man's beard. His breath was scented by hard apple cider. "We want you to help spread our message of freedom."

Timothy blinked. Did he know this man? Why had he chosen a secret name to mask his true self?

"Why me?" Timothy asked.

Paul snickered. "Let the Tories burn! You can swear to that.

"Tomorrow we deliver our sermon by torchlight. We know a farmer who will be warmed by our words." Paul grinned. The crowd buzzed with bursts of hard, sharp laughter.

Those words! That ringing voice! Those words had jolted Timothy from his sleep not so long ago.

Those same words spelled the end of Timothy's parents. Now, Timothy faced the choice of his life.

He looked about the room. British soldiers might think the church was enjoying large numbers for an evening service. He even spied a few men clutching Bibles. That helped hide the real meaning of the protest meeting.

"Shall 'Join or Die' become our group motto?" Patriot Paul asked the group. Laughs popped and crackled like growing flames.

Paul then turned to Timothy. "You can take the 'lie' out of Lyman, boy! Become a man. Save your family name. Bring them honor for once."

Timothy wished to spit in the face of this devil. Instead, Timothy's face matched the look of Patriot Paul's. He copied the jagged smile and all.

"I am grateful, sir," he answered. He spoke loud enough for the entire room

to hear. "I will save my family name. And I will lead your march. You have shown me the way. I will show Tories the light!"

Every man stomped the hard dirt floor. Each pumped fists in the air. The cheers pounded Timothy's ears.

"One more night. Freedom burns bright!" they chanted.

"Meet here at twilight tomorrow," Paul called. "I will show you the way. Then we can show the way to our unfaithful neighbor."

Timothy aimed his hate at Paul. He had fooled the leader. Timothy would welcome the chance to stop the man who had killed his parents.

Chapter 7

Getting Even

The day passed happily for Timothy. Thoughts of revenge filled his mind. They made weeding the garden more pleasant.

Timothy planned his attack. Could Paul be pushed into a flaming house? Could the laughing demon die from a rock to the back of the head?

That night, Parson Worthy said a long prayer of thanks before beginning the meal. Then the Worthys said almost nothing to each other. Only

quick grunts of "Hot?" "Yes." "More?" "No!" could be heard.

Mrs. Worthy had made "garden porridge," a muddy cabbage soup. But it went down painlessly for Timothy.  He floated chunks of stale bread in the boring liquid.

This might be Timothy's last real meal. He would probably flee to the woods after attacking Patriot Paul.

Timothy faked a yawn. Then he stood.

"Pardon me, please," he announced. "I wish to be excused. I will say prayers. And then I will prepare hay for my sleep in the barn. If I may."

Mrs. Worthy jumped from the table. She dug through a cedar chest in the corner of the room.

"Sleep with this," she said.

She placed a thick woolen blanket in Timothy's arms.

He gave a small, true smile to the woman. He gulped as a tear slid down his cheek. "I thank you heartily, ma'am."

Mrs. Worthy shook her head and stared at the floor. "Good night, Timothy. The Lord bless and keep you."

Timothy walked outside. He hugged the blanket. But he wished he were hugging Mrs. Worthy.

Timothy felt ashamed. He had taken the three flags she had sewn with the women. He hoped someday she would forgive him.

Outside the barn, Timothy heard the mob drawing near. He ran. But he did not run away this time. He ran to meet them.

The church disappeared from view. Patriot Paul relayed the call, "To the Blackburns'!"

Wrapped in his blanket, Timothy stopped. The Blackburns lived on the neighboring farm! He knew Matthew.

The boy was Timothy's age. Like Timothy's parents, Matthew's parents had seen all but one child die as babies.

The throng of torchbearers marched past a pile of blackened stone and timber. It was all that was left of Timothy's home. But no one except Timothy remembered.

In minutes, everyone reached the Blackburns' front door.

"Come out, Blackburn trash!" rang out from the darkness.

Timothy gripped a broomstick topped with a flaming rag. He smiled. He knew that Matthew and his parents were smart. They would pretend not to be home.

No! Timothy thought. He saw a candle flickering inside. Then it dimmed. Timothy knew the mob would not quit now.

Chapter 8

Facing a Mob

$\mathcal{P}$atriot Paul renewed his call, "Let the Tories burn!" Those haunting words drove Timothy to action.

He jumped onto a tree stump. "Wait, I beg you!" he shouted. "Let me prove my loyalty. I will call out the Blackburns. Then they will see how we deal with traitors. Let them see our rage. Wait for my signal."

Paul dismounted his horse. He pointed his torch at Timothy. "Lyman, make good on your promise."

"Your kind must learn. Teach them. Just remember—a lie again and you will join your parents!"

Timothy nodded. He turned and swung his torch over his head. "Mister Blackburn. I am your former neighbor," he shouted. "Make way for me."

The door opened a crack. Timothy pushed it open with his foot. The bystanders cheered. Timothy entered.

After a moment, the door flung open wide. "See three faces of freedom. Our newest supporters!" Timothy shouted.

Slowly, he emerged from the home. He was followed by a man, a woman, and a boy. Each was draped in a new American flag. These were the flags Timothy had helped make.

"Do you dare destroy our flag? Our symbol?" Timothy cried. "Destroy the Blackburns and destroy our future!"

A standoff brewed. Timothy and the Blackburn family faced the angry men and their torches.

The four stood with their backs against the house. They knew no escape.

Then a carriage rumbled down the path. "Stop!" cried a woman's voice.

"Timothy, don't move!" shouted a man.

The parson and his wife leaped from the buggy. Mrs. Worthy ran to Timothy and hugged him.

"This boy stands for freedom," Mrs. Worthy said. "He stands for right. Do not stand against us. I speak to the truth and fairness in all of you. Let us work together for freedom."

One by one, torches were snuffed in the dirt. Mr. Blackburn knelt beside Timothy.

"God bless America," he cried. "And God bless you, Master Lyman."

Paul dropped his torch. "A pox on you all!" he swore as he rode away.

As he left, so did the cloud of hatred. Men shuffled away. They left only a weeping Mrs. Blackburn and her family.

Timothy turned to wave at his friends. Parson Worthy called him to a halt.

"I am proud of you, Timothy," he said. "We worried over you. You left as our guest. You will return as our son."

Without another word, the three left for home. They were free and together.

Chapter 9

Friends and Foes

What's a Tory? Who were the Tories?

By 1775, 2.5 million people lived in the 13 colonies. But only about 100,000 people lived in cities.

The rest lived in rural homes. They fished, lumbered, mined, and farmed.

Colonial America • 1775

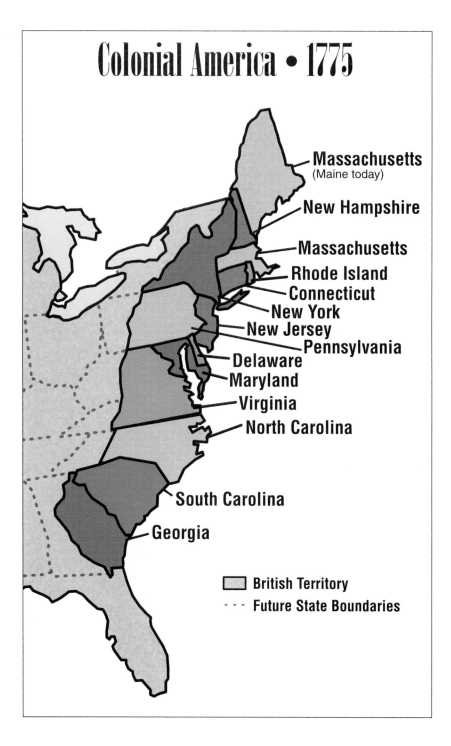

Massachusetts
(Maine today)

New Hampshire

Massachusetts

Rhode Island

Connecticut

New York

New Jersey

Pennsylvania

Delaware

Maryland

Virginia

North Carolina

South Carolina

Georgia

British Territory
- - - Future State Boundaries

They grew rice, tobacco, and **indigo**.

Indigo is a plant used to make a blue dye to color cloth.

Many of these people or their relatives were from **Great Britain**. About one third of the English colonists supported the British government. They were called *Tories*.

The word *Tory* comes from the 17th century. It described country bandits in Ireland.

Great Britain also had a political party named "Tory." But colonists who favored their old country preferred to be called *Loyalists*.

Great Britain is also called England.

Many colonists did not take sides in the war because of their religion. One peaceful group was the Quakers. They felt they could live

their own lives under any government.

Some Tories feared becoming fighters. Choosing one side could bring revenge by the other. **Arson** was an easy way to scare many people. Not just those caught in it. But others who saw it.

Arson is setting a fire on purpose.

Hangings happened too. Along with threats from the famed "Committee of Tarring and Feathering."

This torture was real and deadly.

Posters signed by this group would warn citizens against helping the British.

Tales were common. Hot tar was poured on a stripped Loyalist. That was followed by a shower of feathers. They stuck to the tar. Some rebels even tried to set the feathers on fire.

Sometimes, Tories would be tied to, or dangled from, a tall "Liberty Pole." Others would be chased out of town and their property taken.

Some families split up because of their beliefs. One parent would be for freedom. The other would support English rule. Often, children would be blamed for the actions or ideas of their parents.

Rebels could see the **redcoats** and fight them. But Tories were a silent enemy. They were more feared.

When the rebels marched into a town, townspeople were careful. Many would not tell which side they supported.

Rebels were the colonists who fought for freedom.

Redcoats were the British troops. They were named for the red coats they wore.

Often, the Tory response would be to spy.

They would hear what the rebels were
planning. Then they would find a
nearby British camp. They would pass
on what they knew.

Chapter 10

Stars and Stripes

$\mathscr{A}$t first, each colony was seen as its own country. Each had its own flag.

On June 14, 1777, the second Continental Congress chose a new flag. It would have red and white

Colonial Flag of Rhode Island

stripes and white stars on a blue background.

Would the stripes run side to side or up and down? Which stripe should come first, the red or the white?

Only the idea of one stripe and one star for each of the 13 colonies was decided. That is all Congress agreed upon. No one knew any details.

Surprisingly, only a handful of newspapers printed tiny mentions of a new flag. And that wasn't until September!

One common flag was needed for America's ships.

Ships needed to know where another ship was from. Was it a friend or enemy?

In 1851, Emanuel Leutze finished a famous painting. It showed General Washington crossing the Delaware River on Christmas Day, 1776.

The new flag is flying in the boat. But that was six months before Congress chose the flag!

Did patriots really make their own flags? Maybe. After all, there wasn't a store to buy flags from.

Even if patriots didn't get the colors or design perfect, they wanted some symbol to show they were a part of the fight for freedom.

Today June 14 is remembered. It is a holiday for all Americans. Flag Day.

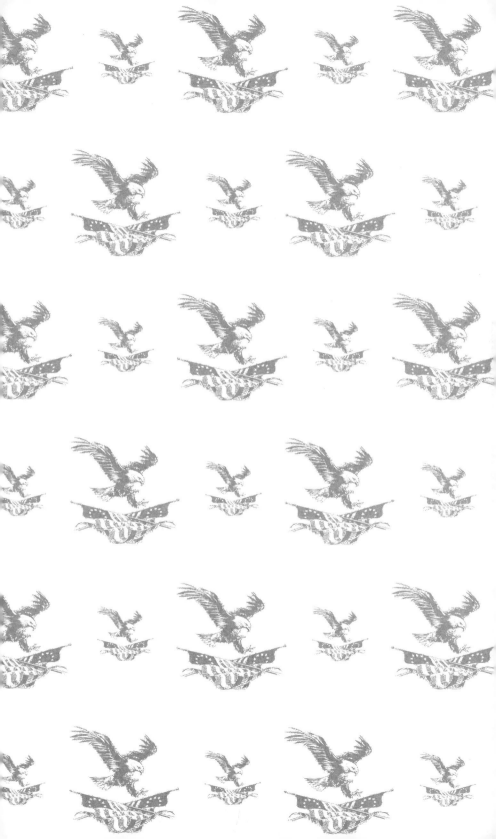